# The Other Side of the Door

## A Collection of Ghost Stories

### Rhonda Parrish

Poise and Pen Publishing
ALBERTA

PoiseAndPen.Com

Publisher's Note: This is a work of fiction. Names, characters, places, and incidents are a product of the author's imagination. Locales and public names are sometimes used for atmospheric purposes. Any resemblance to actual people, living or dead, or to businesses, companies, events, institutions, or locales is completely coincidental.

Cover design by Jonathan C. Parrish
Cover image licensed from Fotolia.com

Book Layout ©2017 BookDesignTemplates.com

The Other Side of the Door/ Rhonda Parrish. — 1st ed.
ISBN 978-1-988233-52-9 (electronic)
ISBN 978-1-988233-53-6 (physical)

# ALSO BY RHONDA PARRISH

## WRITTEN BY
APHANASIAN STORIES
WHITE NOISE
WASTE NOT (AND OTHER FUNNY ZOMBIE STORIES)
STARRY NIGHT
HAUNTED HOSPITALS (CO-WRITTEN WITH MARK LESLIE)

## EDITED BY
A IS FOR APOCALYPSE
B IS FOR BROKEN
C IS FOR CHIMERA
D IS FOR DINOSAUR
E IS FOR EVIL

FAE
CORVIDAE
SCARECROW
SIRENS
EQUUS

FIRE: DEMONS, DRAGONS AND DJINNS

MRS. CLAUS: NOT THE FAIRY TALE THEY SAY

METASTASIS
NITEBLADE MAGAZINE

## COMING SOON
F IS FOR FAIRY
GRIMM, GRIT AND GASOLINE: AN ANTHOLOGY OF
DIESELPUNK AND DECOPUNK FAIRY TALES
EARTH: GIANTS, GOLEMS AND GARGOYLES
HEAR ME ROAR
HOLLOW
SWASHBUCKLING CATS: NINE LIVES ON THE SEVEN SEAS
EERIE EDMONTON

# Contents

# Author's Note

These are not happy stories. Some of them contain depictions of violence, including acts perpetrated against children. Further, most of the characters in these stories do not go on to live happily ever after. If that is going to be problematic for you, proceed with caution.

# The Other Side of the Door

The hockey card pinned to Aric's spokes clattered as he pedaled over the last few yards of his driveway. As he dismounted and leaned the bicycle up against the house he knew it was going to be a bad night. His father's truck was parked crookedly in the driveway with the door open and making a soft dinging sound. After checking through the window to make sure his father wasn't slumped over the seat snoring, Aric slammed the door. The dinging stopped and the cab light went out. Last week when he'd discovered the truck in a similar state he'd left it as it was and the battery had died. His father had been furious and Aric had been unable to sit on his bicycle seat for two days.

As he left the bright sunlight and stepped into the dim light of the house, Aric stopped to give his eyes a moment to adjust. The first thing he recognized as the grey blurs in front of him coalesced into solid objects was the six pack of Ranier longnecks on the kitchen table. Each was empty and had its cap turned up like a crown on its mouth. The air was heavy with their scent and the sharp odor of sweat. An ocean breeze ruffled the curtain of the open kitchen window bringing a small breath of freshness which the house quickly swallowed up.

"That you boy?" his father growled from the cave-like living room. Before his mother died that room had been Aric's favourite in the whole house. Its walls were white with bright yellow trim and the hardwood floor was always swept until it shone. All his mother's bookcases were in there and she had let him read anything he wanted, not just the little kid books. He'd spent hours curled up on the soft couch consuming the words of writers as diverse as A.A. Milne, Ray Bradbury, Stephen King and Beatrix Potter.

No longer.

Now the walls were stained with tobacco smoke, and the stink of cigarettes clouded the air even in their absence. The floor was worn and grungy, and Aric's feet often stuck to it when he walked across. Worst of all, that's where the stairs were.

"Boy?" His father said again, and Aric considered fleeing out the back door and pretending he'd never been there, but the screen door's squeak would give him away and then he'd be in for it.

"Yes, it's me."

"Where you bin?"

"With Austin," Aric answered truthfully. "Down on the beach."

Their house was the last one on the bay before open water and ever since Austin and his family had moved in just down the road, he and Aric had been inseparable. They played on the rocky coastline for hours. Looking in tide pools, skipping rocks and having adventures. Austin was his best friend, the only person in the world he'd even *considered* talking to about his mother. Of course, in the end he'd decided against that. It was safer that way. For everyone.

In the living room, his father made a non-committal grunt and turned his attention back to the baseball game showing on the cabinet television he'd dragged in from the garage. Aric could remember his parents fighting about it. His father wanted it in the house but his mother didn't, she said television rotted the mind. It was the one argument Aric could ever remember his mother winning. Assuming she had, that is. Which wasn't an assumption he could safely make since the television had been in the house before his mother had even been in the ground.

He looked at the floor. Cigarette ashes and scattered burn marks marred its worn surface. He used to be bothered by that, but right now the only thing bothering him was the grumbling in his stomach. He was hungry. He hadn't eaten anything but the piece of dry toast he'd snatched on his way out the door this morning, and he'd spent all day being a pirate with Austin. Pillaging and sword fighting built up an appetite. Still, given the six 'dead soldiers' on the kitchen table and the half-consumed one in his father's hand, it might be better to go to bed now and try to sneak down for a snack later, after his dad fell asleep in his chair.

"What you loomin' there for?" his father snarled.

Caught by surprise Aric blurted out the first thing that came to mind, the truth. "I'm hungry."

"I'm hungry," his father said, lifting his voice high in a mockery of Aric's. "I'm hungry. Well I'm damned tired so why don't *you* cook us somethin' for a change?"

Aric was doing his best to fry up some eggs and potatoes when he heard the ominous crunch of gravel under tires. His father heard it too. He was up and swearing, stumbling past Aric and toward the kitchen door before the car was even stopped. "Goddamn it, why don't those bastards leave me alone?" He said, scratching at the graying hair on his chest.

Glancing out the window Aric saw Officer Perkin's RCMP car. He looked down at the food in the frying pan. "They want to talk to you about Mama again?"

Crack!

Aric felt the weight of the back of his father's hand across the side of his face. It knocked him clean off the chair he'd been standing on to use the stove and left him sprawled across the cracked linoleum floor. Tears sprung to his eyes but he blinked them back. He would not cry. He would not. Crying always made it worse.

Outside, the car pulled to a stop and Aric heard the door squeak open. The sound was of metal on metal, a terrible squeal like something from a scary book. He looked up to see his father's finger pointing at him. "Get up to your room and don't let me hear a peep from you or you'll regret it."

Aric scrambled to his feet and up the stairs to his room. His cheek throbbed and burned. He didn't have a mirror but he imagined the hurt took the shape of his father's hand, and when he held his own near it he could feel warmth radiate off it. His eyes burned as though he'd been crying though he hadn't shed a tear.

His window faced out into the bay, so he couldn't see his father and Officer Perkins talking, but he could guess at the conversation. Ever since his mother died the police had come around a lot. His father said it had been an accident, claimed she'd tripped over one of Aric's toys and tumbled down the stairs. But Aric knew better. He'd heard the fight that happened right beforehand. Truthfully it hadn't been better or worse than any of the million fights they'd had before, not until the sudden ending.

"...takin' him and leaving!" His mother had screamed, her voice shrill and cracking. It was a sentiment he'd heard over and over for years, one that made him burrow deeper into his quilt, trying to block out the sound because it always resulted in his father getting even angrier. And he had. He'd roared like a fog horn and from his room Aric had heard him stomp down the hallway toward where his mother stood at the top of the stairs. And then there had been the crash. And her scream. Her scream that went on and on for an impossibly long time. And then there was silence.

Aric's dad talked to Officer Perkins, now as he had then, and sent him on his way. There was no ambulance following in his wake on this trip, but he was gone just the same. Aric heard his father slam the door as he came back in from talking on the driveway, and then, from all the way upstairs, he heard the unmistakable sound of his dad twisting the top off another Ranier and throwing the cap on the table.

Aric tracked his father's progress through the house by the sound of his heavy boots on the floor. He paced around the kitchen some, grumbling and muttering. Then came the crash of the frying pan Aric had been using being thrown into the kitchen sink. "Burnin' food, ye little bastard!" his father yelled up the stairs. "I'm gonna take the cost a that outta yer ass!"

His father took the steps two at a time, his work boots coming down on them hard enough Aric wondered if one might break and grant him a reprieve. The sound hammered in Aric's chest and nausea twisted his guts into a bowline knot.

Bang.

Bang.

Bang.

Then he was there and the knob on the door was twisting, the door opening.

He filled the door frame, blocking out nearly all the light from the hallway so the little which did manage to penetrate cloaked him like a halo. His chest heaved, shoulders rising and falling like whitecaps, and the scent of beer filled the room. "Gonna pay for that boy. Ye think we can afford to waste food? Huh? Or maybe ye were tryin' to burn the place down, eh? That it?"

"No sir," Aric backed up into the shadows of his bed. Hunching his shoulders and folding as much of himself inward as he could. Trying to become small, so small his father wouldn't notice him anymore. As small as a mouse, as a bug. As small as he felt. "I'm sorry."

"I'm sorry. I'm sorry. You're always sorry." His father roared, spittle spraying from his lips as he stepped toward Aric. "Sorry just doesn't cut it! You've. Got. To. Learn. To. Think!"

His father backhanded him and the pain bloomed fierce and white as he tumbled to the floor and scrunched his eyes shut to hide from what was coming. Then his father was there, picking him up by the shoulders and shaking him, and shaking him and shaking—

When Aric opened his eyes he was lying beneath the patchwork quilt on his bed. His father wasn't there and the house was dark. He lay perfectly still, listening. If his father heard him get out of bed he might come back up and well, Aric might be joining his mother in her burial at sea. And sometimes, sometimes he thought maybe that wasn't such a bad idea. He'd read stories about heaven and thought it sounded like a mighty nice place to go, but still, he wasn't sure. What if the stories were wrong?

So he waited.

But the house was quiet except for the familiar tick-tock of the old clock out in the hall.

And then for no reason he could think of, except that it suddenly seemed like a very good idea, Aric got out of bed. He tiptoed across his room, careful to miss the squeaky board by his dresser, pulled the lace curtains back from the window and squinted into the mist.

The boat was carried in on the back of the fog.

Growing up on the bay, Aric had seen boats slip through fog plenty of times, he'd even been on a few of them. They were nothing new or unusual for him, and yet—there was something about the shape in the mist, about this particular vessel. He leaned closer and pressed his forehead against the glass.

The shape tickled his brain. It didn't feel solid. It kept shifting in the fog so that he couldn't tell how big it was let alone what kind of craft. One moment it looked like a sailboat, the next its silhouette was that of a scallop dragger. It was as if it were being formed and reformed by the fog's icy fingers while he watched.

As the tide brought it nearer, Aric saw that, in fact, it was a rowboat. An empty rowboat.

Empty, and yet he could hear the soft splash of the boat's oars entering the water, the whoosh of it cutting through the bay toward him and then the trickle of droplets running down the oars and back into the sea.

Aric was filled, not with fear, but excitement, as he watched the little dory come closer. The name *SOUNDER* was scrawled across her bow, and the black words shone in the moonlight as though they were painted with reflective paint. In, the oars went, and then back, pulled by invisible arms, and out and in. The water droplets fell off them like diamonds, leaving ripples in the surface of the ocean that spread out as far as Aric could see. In and out.

The boat ran up against the stony shore below their house and the oars tucked themselves neatly inside.

It should have been impossible for Aric to see the rocks shift as though they were being walked on, or for him to hear their crunch against one another, but he could. As clearly as if he were watching a movie. And still, even as he tracked the invisible being's progress toward him, Aric was not afraid. It was only when the steps went around the corner of the house where the door was and Aric could no longer see them, that he became anxious. Did he dare risk his father's wrath by going downstairs to see where the ghost was going? Because he was certain it was a ghost – what else could it be?

His decision was made for him when he heard the door open. The ghost moved about the kitchen some, and then he heard it coming up the stairs. Slowly. Deliberately. Heading toward his room.

Shouldn't a ghost be silent, he thought, and then first trickles of fear ran down his spine, spreading their tingling fingers all through his body and he pressed his back against the far wall.

And then he knew. As suddenly and surely as he'd known to go to the window and look out, Aric knew who was on the other side of the door. He ran toward it, reaching it just as it was opened and threw himself into his mother's arms.

He could see her, feel her, could smell her. More real, more alive than anything else around him. He felt his tears wet her shoulder, smelled the faint scent of her favourite bubble bath mingling with that of the night air which clung to her. Her arms were warm around him, and her breath stirred his hair.

"Mommy," he breathed, pulling away just enough to look into her face, to see the tears and the smile there. "I missed you."

"I missed you too, Aric," she said, smoothing his hair down in back, blinking away tears. "But now it's time to go."

Aric opened his mouth to question, to dispute, then followed his mother's gaze to his bed. Tucked away in the corner and painted with shadows though it was, still he could see. He could see the truth. The stiff form lying beneath the blanket. Hands folded over its chest. With a cry he turned away, burying himself in his mother's arms once more.

She carried him down the stairs, though he was far too big for that, and as they passed through the living room Aric heard a foreign sound. The thick, wet sound of his father crying, sobbing in the darkness. "I'm sorry," he said, over and over, his voice slurred from beer, heavy with tears. "I'm so, so sorry."

Aric looked up to see his father sitting in his usual chair, his face buried in his hands, shoulders convulsing. "Sorry just doesn't cut it," Aric whispered, and it felt right, and good. For a moment. Then remorse washed over him, and guilt, like a tide, and he tightened his grip around his mother's neck.

She stepped out of the house, with him in her arms, about the same time the night sky was painted with red and blue lights from Officer Perkin's car.

Outside beneath the stars, his mother set Aric on his feet. He looked toward the shore where the little skiff waited and slipped his hand into hers. They took their first step toward it together.

# Cold Comfort

It was bitterly cold. Bethany's nostrils froze together with each inhalation and her eyelashes clung to one another when she blinked. She'd been walking through the snow a long time. Her thighs felt as though a thousand icy needles pierced them and her boots like anvils.

The blizzard had come out of nowhere, blinding her completely but Bethany knew they were almost home so she did her best to keep the horse pointed toward home and her heels in his sides. However, once the worst of the storm had passed it was clear they were in the middle of the woods, the worn track they'd been traveling on nowhere in sight. The storm had covered up their tracks so Bethany pointed the horse toward where the drifts seemed the lowest and pushed him forward. As daylight perished the horse had stumbled and refused to rise and now, many hours later, Bethany was sorely tempted to do the same.

And then she saw it.

The cottage filled the opening between the spruce trees, like something out of a fairy tale. Snow pillowed upon its roof but golden light poured out through its windows like honey.

She ran, stumbling in the knee-high drifts, and fell, palms first, into the snow. Her hands, bare, red and raw, burned from the cold and as she trudged the rest of the way to the cabin, she breathed clouds of warmth against them to soothe the pain.

The window glass was clear as crystal and through it Bethany could see the roaring fire in the fireplace, a tree bedecked with ornaments with a blanket of brightly wrapped gifts at its feet. A child sat between the tree and the pane, staring back at her through the barrier. A blue-eyed darling with golden ringlets and a sugary smile. A smile which widened as Bethany approached. The girl leaped up, gesturing excitedly toward the door.

As she trudged through the drifts to join her Bethany could almost feel the warmth of the fire. Almost. She glanced up at the stars, shining brighter than ever she'd seen them, and thanked the Lord for delivering her from the cold. For bringing her to safety.

Then she noticed the chimney.

It was straight as Jesus' cross, and the moon lit it well enough for her to see the stones used to build it, but no smoke escaped its mouth. No clouds, like those which fogged the air before her, spilled from its lip.

Confused, fingers numb and mind slowed as well, she continued around the corner, toward the door the girl had pointed to.

And there it was, flying open and spilling golden light and cheerful sound out onto the snow. "Come on, come on," the girl laughed and beckoned with her hand. No fog surrounded her either, nor did any pour from the doorway.

Bethany hesitated. She stepped forward and the little girl's eyes twinkled. Twinkled with something that had naught to do with being jolly and everything to do with hunger.

Hunger like Bethany felt for the warmth the cottage promised. Desperate and toothy.

She took another step. She could see the fire dancing behind the girl, could hear it crackle and pop, but though she was near enough to reach out and touch the door frame, she could not feel even a hint of its warmth.

"Come on," the girl said. "Come in!"

Bethany looked from the child, alone in the cabin lit with gold and cheer, then back to the wood where looming trees boughs were twisted into claws and their moonshadows reached toward her. Better, she thought, to spend the night in Winter's embrace than whatever was in that house.

Bethany took a step backward, and the girl-thing frowned. Then she took another, and another. Its features twisted into something feral, something hungry. "Come in," it said once more, but this time the snarl hidden beneath its words was loud in Bethany's ears, and the next step backward was easier to take than the ones which came before.

Crossing herself, Bethany turned her back on the girl-thing and the cottage and a howl, frustrated and fierce, echoed through the woods. And when, eventually, she dared look back over her shoulder, the cottage was gone with no sign that it had ever been.

# A Voice Too Many

Widow Crocker's in the kitchen
baking today's bread
and Sally is in my chambers
making up the bed.

Sally snaps my bed sheets
and hums a mournful tune
all about a soldier boy
and his cursed platoon.

Her mother's joyful song floats
from the floor below,
accompanied by the heavy sound
of her punching in the dough.

The three of us ought be
alone in the chateau
yet from *her* room I hear—oh!
I don't even want to know.

It sounds just like the rocking chair,
the song she used to sing
when I was but a babe-in-arms
she, lover of the king.

But then she made him angry
and the old man claimed her head.
So how can I hear her singing, singing?
When she is long since dead.

# A Million Pieces

They say it's the things which drove you crazy that you miss the most. I never much believed it myself. Not until I lost you.

It's been a year now. And what a year. A year of rehab and therapy, lawyers and courtrooms. A year of firsts

My first surgery. First steps without my walker. First birthday without you. First day back in our apartment, alone. First night—

So many things you could have counted. So. Many.

It used to frustrate me so much, your counting, but my love was deeper than my irritation so I stayed. Stayed though you counted every Cheerio in your bowl. All the bowls in the cupboard. Every spoon.

I loved you enough to stay though you counted your pills six times a day. And when you stopped taking them? I stayed then too.

Our last Valentine's Day we spent, me dressed up, crying and watching you crawl across the floor in your suit picking up each Q-tip from the Costco-sized box I'd spilled and counting, counting, counting.

I stayed through all that, yet you let a drunk driver tear you from me. One. One care. One driver. One crash.

Christmas was always your favourite holiday, and I'm celebrating in style in honor and remembrance of you. I've baskets full of Christmas balls scattered throughout the house. Festive decorations, and the tree is up and decorated. I think you'd approve. The lights twinkling on it are reflected in the glass globes which adorn it and nearby the fireplace snaps and pops. Outside, snow is falling, piling up in the corners of our windows, and my want for you is so intense it's nearly a physical thing.

I stare out at the city. From this high up all I see is a sea of lights piecing the darkness. Like stars.

I look up, then, expecting to be disappointed; stars-watching and snowfall so rarely go together, but through a clearing in the clouds, just to the left of the moon, one star gleams. It's super bright and though I don't know its name or if it's a part of a constellation, I'd bet it's one sailors use to navigate. To find their way back home.

I close my eyes.

I make a wish.

When I open them, something has changed. Not outside. The moon and star are still there, snow still falls and below steams of red taillights still move alongside the blue-white of halogen headlights.

I shift my focus from beyond the window, to its glass. The change is in here. With us. The window reflects the room back at me. Tree, fireplace, me...and you.

Your reflection as solid as mine. Distorted ever so slightly by the flaws in the glass, but distinctly you. Your shaggy hair. Your hipster glasses. Your mouth which moves, your voice I hear.

"I missed you—" You reach for me. You reach for me and I panic and grab the basket of Christmas balls from the window ledge beside me. The wicker is hard against my fingers, unforgiving. I turn it upside down, pour out the balls which tumble over one another, and onto the floor.

You stop. Your graze drops to the floor, then back up to mine, reflected in the window.

"I—" you begin, then stop and chew on the corner of your pinky finger's nail. My chest clenches at the sight, so familiar.

Your indecision is a vacuum sucking all the air from the room, slowing the tick-tock of the clock on the mantle until each sound is a long, drawn-out scream. I can't move. Can't breathe. My eyes burn, but I cannot cry.

"One," you say, kneeling down and disappearing from my sight. "Two—"

I exhale. The grip on my chest loosens and the clock resumes its natural rhythm.

"Three, four..."

How many balls were there? A dozen? More?

Too few. Too few.

I step back and white heat rips through my heel as the ball crunches beneath it.

Blood stains the milky glass shards, drips from my foot to the hardwood. You reach for a piece, a shard, "Five, six, seven..."

A sob catches in my throat and a snatch a ball from the tree. It's blue and glittery, the surface rough against my palm. I remember picking it out with you three years ago. From the antique store we stopped in on our way home from the local theatre's production of A Christmas Carole. You'd grinned at me then, so big I could see the gap between your bottom teeth, and your eyes shone with love. It was a perfect moment in a perfect day.

How many more of those days could we have had?

"Eighteen, nineteen, twenty—"

How many were stolen from me?

"Twenty-four, twenty-five—"

...from us?

"Twenty-seven, twenty-eight, twenty-nine—"

I hurl the glass ball down with all my strength so it shatters. I rip the next from the fir's branches and smash it too. And the next, and the next.

I scream out my anger. I sob out my sorrow. My blood mixes with the fragments of memory spreading across the floor and woven through it all, your voice. Implacable. Counting.

"Three thousand four hundred and two, three thousand four hundred and three—"

# A Coming Storm

My very first raid. The air was redolent with the scent of burned flesh, like bacon. My stomach rumbled and I couldn't be sure if it was because of hunger at the smell, or revulsion at its source. I'd done as I was told, staying back with all the casters until the ungrounded men could shut down the fence and when the bugles rang out I'd charged in with the rest of them. Fingers stiff around the stock of my rifle, thoughts of everything that had led me here at the front of my mind and a cry of rage on my lips.

∽∽∿∼∿

The barn was hot and fragrant with the scent of straw and horseflesh. The mid-afternoon sun filtered in through the rawhide windows and motes and bits of hay twisted and twirled in its beams while James and I melted together then pulled apart, slow and sticky as taffy. Our sighs and moans were muffled, lost in the sounds of the horses stamping and shuffling in their stalls.

"Jeremiah!" my father's booming voice filled the barn and James and I froze, passion turned to fear, arousal wilting like a picked flower in the sun.

*A storm is coming.*

The thought branded itself on my brain. The words a code between my sister, Amy, and I. Words that would send her running to hide in the old hollow tree in the woods behind our home. A storm was coming, but for James and I there was no easy escape. No secret hiding place.

"What?" I yelled back, trying to keep the fear and passion out of my voice. To act normal just in case he was here for a reason other than to discover us. Just in case the storm could be avoided.

James scurried into the corner of the stall, laying flat on his back and scooping great armfuls of straw over himself. I would have helped but I was too busy digging my clothes out of the straw and shoving limbs into them. All for naught.

Father raged down the length of the barn, spooking the horses so that they whinnied and reared in their stalls. When he rounded the corner and saw James and I, stricken and so obviously *together*, the storm erupted.

Father said it would hurt him more than it did me, but his eyes were flint when he tied me to the whipping post and his strikes swift and sure. The whip's kiss was fire, searing my skin and opening my back so blood ran down it to soak my breeches.

"A caster!" he spat the word like rattlesnake venom as he coiled the dripping whip around his fist. "My own son fucking a goddamned magi!"

He left me bound all the rest of the day to bleed the evil out of me and that night, in the darkness, he punished James the same way I had loved him. Night was my blindfold but I could hear. He made goddamned sure I could hear.

In the morning when my brother Abe cut me down his eyes were red and swollen. He cried. Said his tears were because he loved me, wanted only good for me, only what was right. What was natural.

Love was natural, I told him, my voice as cracked as the scabs covering my back.

Not, he said, love between a man and a magi. Couldn't I see? Couldn't I?

I could not.

Clarence was a magi, grounded like so many of his kind so that he could only wield shot, not spells. On that day, my first raid, I never even fired my rifle. The homesteader and his family ran after they saw what our magi did to their hired hands whose charred bodies were twisted into grotesque shapes scattered about the farmyard. They didn't get far. The man and his son were executed on the spot, the wife would be let go after. After...

All the magi slaves were released, welcome to add their number to our ranks or go off on their own. Most joined up because where could they go?

Clarence's accident happened as the ungrounded magi were destroying the outbuildings. I was watching, fascinated. I'd heard magi could boil air and throw fire but hadn't ever seen it until then. The caster, a girl no older than Amy, stood staring at the barn with an intensity that was almost sexual. Her lips were moving, and though I was too far away to hear her words I felt their power. The hair on my arms stood on end and my chest tingled.

A ball of flame appeared between her hands, twisting and growing. Spinning and humming. Soon it was the size of a cat, then a dog. By the time it was as big as a horse the girl's hair and robes were flowing back behind her and the roar of the flames was like a locomotive in my ears. She thrust her hands forward and threw the ball into the barn. The barn which was a building one moment and a burning pile of rubble the next.

Between the two events there was an explosion and Clarence, standing far too near the barn, was tossed forward like a ragdoll, back bent into a C, then he was yanked back into the inferno. It was like a nightmare — everything was in slow motion but I was unable to act. I watched his eyes grow wide, his mouth open in a scream that was lost in the fire's song.

I saw him get jerked into the hungry flames then watched his ghost run back out again.

Clarence's ghost looked just like him only less solid. I couldn't see through him like a pane of glass, but he wasn't all there either. Like a fog. I saw, or imagined I did, the shadows from the fires moving through him and swore under my breath.

"You ain't never seen no one in flux before, boy?"

I hadn't. I'd heard it happened but I guess I'd always assumed it was an old wife's tale, a story told to frighten children.

"Wow. That was close, eh Jeremiah?" Clarence's ghost called, relief evident in his voice, his step, as he ran toward us.

Lost for a response I forced a smile and waved at him, then turned to the old timer beside me. I didn't like him. His name was John. John Gordon, and other than the side he was on he reminded me very much of my father.

"He doesn't know?"

"Nope," the old man spat on the ground then met my gaze. "Knew one fluxed soul once, didn't realise he was dead for three whole days. Three days, can you imagine?"

I could. I didn't want to, but I could.

Father was not finished.

Abe brought me, oozing, staggering and broken back to the barn, to the scene of my "crime". I went meekly, sagging against my brother despite his betrayal, in order to remain on my feet. Then I saw her and I knew what Father planned.

I swear my heart stopped for a moment, then raced as fast as a rat's to make up for it. I could hear the blood rushing through my ears, smell the piss that ran down my leg.

"No," I said. "No, you can't possibly mean to—"

"I do." Father's voice, from behind me.

I twisted as much as my back would allow to face him, slipped from Abe's grip and tumbled to my knees in the straw. All my hate for my father, all the venom I felt for what he'd done to me and to James was swept away, swallowed by fear. "Father, don't! You can't—"

"I can and will," he looked at me, pitiless. "Your mother, may she rest in peace, would want me to save you from yourself. To salvage your soul, even at the expense of your body."

"You're going to ground me?" I cried, looking back over my shoulder at the woman waiting there.

I didn't know her name, just that she was the only person in all the state who performed groundings. Father called her in every time he acquired a new slave. I'd seen her around. I'd heard the screams which she worked. I'd seen the end results.

"God be good," Father said, drawing my gaze back to him, "the iron will absorb the evil within you the same way it does the magic in the magi."

"Laudanum?" the woman asked. "I charge extra."

The volume of the tears coursing down my cheeks doubled as Father shook his head.

"I'll pay," Abe said, reaching down to help me to my feet once more. "He's only sixteen Father, barely a man. I'll pay for it."

A rush of gratitude shook me as I grasped his arm and helped him pull me up. I wanted very much to hate him but I couldn't just then. I couldn't.

He and Father looked at one another for a very long moment and then, eventually, Father shrugged. "Your money, your call."

He coughed a ball of phlegm up and spat it in the corner of the stall before looking at me once more. Bleeding, crying and covered in my own piss I must have been a pitiful sight, but my old man looked at me like I was a louse or a June bug he'd just scraped off the bottom of his boot.

"Once yer healed up you'll leave. I won't have no one saying I sent ye out to die, but I won't harbour a magi-lover beneath my roof either. I won't."

"I hate you," I said.

"Then I'm doing something right," he spat once more then turned on his heel and walked out of the barn.

And so I was drugged to oblivion when I was grounded. I didn't feel the knife slicing into my chest, wasn't conscious as the nameless woman, her heart as hard as the metal she worked with, implanted three iron bars inside me.

In a magi the iron dulled or absorbed their magic, making them as powerless as a normal man. More so, even, because the bars were always placed deep, behind major veins or arteries, and homesteaders like my father ringed their properties with magnetic fence lines; powerful magnets hooked up to gas generators to boost their strength. For most men they have no effect except perhaps for a headache, but for someone who is grounded... They rip the bars from our flesh, stealing our lives with them.

I pressed my hand against my chest. I could feel the iron there, or imagined I could. I looked up at John Gordon once more and something in my face wiped the smile off his.

"The iron, it absorbs more than just magic. It—ah hell, I don' t know. Maybe you'll be lucky, boy," he pointed over to Clarence whose ghostly form was dissipating like leaves in a windstorm.

"Maybe you'll be lucky like your friend there and only be in flux a short while."

I could barely breath. I felt like I'd been punched in the gut. I felt dizzy. I turned away from the old timer, from Clarence. How had I gone so long without knowing? We'd had grounded magi slaves the whole time I was growing up. How had I never seen anyone in flux before? Had Abe? Had Amy?

⌁

I spent several days lost to fever and several more to the laudanum Abe provided to dull my pain. I could lie on neither my back or my front and had to stay on my side or propped in a seated position the entire time. When, eventually, I became aware of my surroundings again the first person I recognised was Amy.

Amy.

Amy who, since our mother died had been too shy to speak to anyone but me and even then never above a whisper, was the one to nurse me back to health. Amy, who came into my room every day and mopped at the seeping wounds on my back. Amy whose breath stirred the hair around my ear when she whispered to me that James was gone. That Father had sold him to Fred Jones, a rancher famous for the grounded fist fighting club he ran out of his barn.

Rumor said the losing magi of each fight was sent through the fence and James was a lover, not a fighter.

Amy cradled my head in her hands, only ten years old but she held me while I sobbed and we fell asleep holding one another.

I woke to the sound of Father's boots on the step, the unmistakable heavy tread which meant he was angry, and shook Amy awake.  The bed shifted beneath her as she stretched and I whispered, "A storm is coming." She stiffened, frozen in place for a split second and then she bolted. First toward the door then, hearing Father approach, to my wardrobe. She closed its door behind her with the softest click as the pool of light from Father's lantern poured beneath the door.

Father's body filled the frame and the lantern in his hand threw shadows over his face, distorting his features and making them appear as demonic as they'd been in my fever and pain-filled dreams. He cast his gaze about the room and, seeing no one but me, beheld me steadily. My hands curled into fists. I wanted to hurt him for what he'd done to James. For what he'd done to me. I wanted to hear him scream as James had screamed. To be afraid, to hurt. I wanted to choke him until his face turned purple as a beet and the hate went out of his eyes. But I knew I couldn't.

He had the strength of a bull and I was weak by nature, made weaker by torture. To attack him would be suicidal and he wasn't worth dying for. One day, I would have my revenge but that day was not today.

"You look well enough," he said. "Tomorrow at dawn I'm re-fueling the generators for the fence. They'll be shut down for twenty minutes. Don't be here when they start up again.

I didn't trust myself to speak so I just nodded.

He backed out of the room without looking away from me, like I was something to be feared. I nearly laughed. Nearly. I was weak now but someday I wouldn't be. Someday.

The door closed behind him with a click and his steps retreated down the hall. I counted slowly to twenty after I couldn't hear them anymore, then called to Amy.

"It's okay, you can come out now."

The wardrobe door flew open and a whirlwind of skirts, ribbons and petticoats spun across the room and collapsed upon my bed. I felt her tears hot against my chest and tasted her hair on my lips.

"I don't want you to go," she whispered between sobs.

"I don't have a choice," I said, pulling the strands of her hair from my mouth and stroking her head like I would a cat.

"Take me with you."

My guts twisted. I hated to refuse her anything, especially this thing which meant leaving her here with Father, but I had to. I had to.

When I left there was only one place I could go. I planned to join the Redlegs, the rebels who roamed the countryside of all the states grounding was legal, releasing slaves and punishing their captors; men like my father. That was no life for my lovely sister. My sister who couldn't even speak in the company of others could certainly not rough it with those kind of men. She was safer here.

Father wouldn't hurt her. Not really. She was betrothed to Old Man Williams. A kindly plantation owner, a widower who didn't believe in slavery and so needed lots of sons to work his land. His first wife had given him half a dozen and as soon as Amy was old enough to bleed he would claim her as his own. Her bride price was high enough that rather than risk its loss Father would keep his temper in check.

Life with Old Man Williams wouldn't be glamorous but it would be safe and his property wasn't fenced so perhaps I could even visit. Someday.

I said as much to Amy, holding her while she cried, stroking her hair and silently cursing my father. I wished a thousand deaths upon him, each more painful than the last.

The days ran into one another like water in a stream, only the occasional raid, like a boulder, disrupted the flow. The Redlegs' officers seemed content, more or less, to just exist, to enjoy camp life. It was only when the more rowdy members became restless that they planned another raid.

When I first joined up I'd been sad, mostly, filled with self-pity and loneliness, but as time went on that changed. With each raid I saw how poorly magi were treated. My father, despite what he'd done to James and me, was among one of the better slave owners. Owners. As if one man could own another. But still, at least he provided shelter, food and clothing to his slaves. At least he didn't breed them like cattle or make soap from their corpses.

With each homestead we visited I became angrier. Harder. Colder. My heart was as scarred as my body, as tough. It could not be penetrated and would not hear of mercy.

I became one of the restless. I spent my days pacing around the camp like a caged coyote, my nights staring into flames, missing Amy and James or lost in dreams of vengeance. For myself. For all grounded men.

The Redlegs, imaginatively named for the color our breeches ought be stained from wading through the carnage we left behind, moved in an ever-tightening circle and so it was that as the countryside was on the brink of winter we came to Fred Jones' stead.

When the bugle sounded to signal that the fence was down, and it was safe for the grounded men to advance, my heart was beating like a snare drum. I didn't know if it was for hope of seeing James or fear of it. Either way, my boots had never been heavier, my grip on my rifle tighter or my knuckles more white.

By the time I reached it, the farmyard was already shrouded in arid smoke. True to his nature, Jones had opted to fight, to resist. What's more, he'd apparently hired his own personal guard of magi. Equal parts gunpowder and magic scented the air. I lifted my rifle to my shoulder and began to shoot. I'd been with the Redlegs for long enough to recognise friend from foe even with reduced visibility and in the chaos of the battle, and I was a good shot. Good enough to contribute to our slowly won victory.

Spells shook the tree I'd leaned my rifle against to help steady it, and at one point its boughs caught the still-smoking corpse of a man I'd never seen before, but I didn't let that distract me for long. The corpse couldn't do much to me from beyond the grave and I had to keep firing. Had to make this battle come to an end as quickly as possible so I could get down to the business of finding James, or finding out what had happened to him.

Jones had a big family. I didn't lack for targets.

I loaded and shot. Loaded and shot. Advancing step by step behind our melee fighters once the first barrage was through. Then I saw James, or rather, I saw his ghost.

Before I could even begin to think how to react, he saw me. He smiled and ran toward me through the smoke, arms spread wide. He seemed oblivious to the spells, the gunshots, the chaos, and everyone breathing disregarded him because a bound man poses a threat to no one.

I tried to swallow but it was suddenly very difficult and my throat worked spasmodically to gulp down the giant lump that was wedged within it. I felt my eyes burn, not from the smoke but from the tears that pricked the back of my lids. James was dead. Dead.

I let my rifle drop to my side and reached for him—just as his form began to dissipate. No! I screamed. No, and then no again, but of course that didn't stop him and by the time I reached the spot where he had stood he was gone, leaving me with nothing but the imagined sound of him saying my name among the cacophony of battle around me.

~~~~~~

Dawn came too soon, but as the sky turned from iron to lead I hugged Amy one last time. "Just remember," I said. "Whenever there is a storm coming you need to hide. Just run and hide and don't come out until you know it's safe."

I took one more look around the room that had been mine since the day I was born and then, with nothing more than the clothes on my back and a full canteen, I turned and left. I walked out of my room, away from my home and toward the gate without looking back. I felt Amy's eyes on me the whole way but no one else came to see me off or say goodbye. The property was unnaturally deserted. No house servants could be heard moving about in the kitchens or bedrooms, there was no one in the yard or fields. They were all locked down while the fence was out of commission.

It made my walk even lonelier, my heart harder toward my father. As I approached the fence line I heard a generator cough to life, felt its rumble, like a distant stampede, through the ground. It wasn't the generator which controlled the section of fence nearest me but it was close. I felt the farm closing in around me. Don't be here when they start up again, Father had said, and I wouldn't be.

I picked up my pace and when the fence line nearest to me hummed to life I was a good, safe distance from it. Still, I felt it tug at the iron in my chest, pulling it toward my spine, trying to force me back to the stead.

I stopped at last and looked behind me. I could see my father's bear-like figure silhouetted by the pale morning sun against the backdrop of the only home I'd ever known. I watched him t urn his head to spit before he continued down the line to restart the next generator.

Looking back, I do believe I went mad. That is no excuse but it is the only way I can explain how I could do what I did.

They found Fred barricaded in his home with his family, shooting out through the windows. The fool had obviously never seen what a fireball could do or he'd have taken his chances out in the fields. By the time I reached it, the magi had the house surrounded and were waiting for orders. We all had our backs pressed against the walls of various outbuildings, listening to the thud and whine of bullets slamming into the ground and ricocheting off the wood around us.

We waited.

My hands were clenched tight around my rifle and the blood pounded in my skull. James was dead. Dead. And it was all because of my father. I had despised him for what he'd done to James in the dark, for all that he'd done to me, but now my hatred knew new depths. James was dead. Because of him. My stomach was clenched as though in a fist and my ears buzzed like a hornet's nest.

We waited. And with every beat my heart pumped poison into my body. The feelings I had toward my father, toward myself, as black as tar, worked their way through me. Turning me into someone else.

Rumor was that with winter coming we'd be raiding less and in order to keep peace in the camp for as long as possible the commanders were going to give the rabble-rousers every opportunity to act out, to vent our aggression, to get it out of our systems.

The rumors were right.

Instead of ordering the magi to blow the house up the commanders rounded up a trio of casters and a half dozen melee fighters. The fighters carried the casters between them, steadily toward the house. In that way the magi could still cast while they were moving and though the Jones family shot round after round at the small group not a single one reached their target.

The fighters and magi were soon in control of the house and, unfortunately for the barricaded homesteaders, they took the inhabitants alive.

At that point the commanders mounted up and rode away. Ostensibly they were off to see that all the enslaved magi were released, the wounded tended, but we knew what it really meant. They didn't want to see what was going to happen in that house, but they weren't going to stop it either.

Most of the Redlegs followed their commanders away, but not me. Not me.

On any other day I would have. I don't deceive myself enough to think I would have been brave or noble enough to stop what was happening, but I'd have walked away. But not that day. Not that moment. I had so much anger, so much hate boiling away inside of me that I couldn't. There was only one way to release it.

I walked toward the farmhouse. When the screaming began I picked up my pace until I was running, hell-bent for leather, into that little white homestead.

I didn't rape her. That thought is the one which brings me comfort, but it shouldn't. I didn't rape her but I might as well have. I held the gun on her father, on old Fred Jones, while my brothers in arms took their turns with his daughter. While she screamed and kicked and scratched. I shot him in the knee when he recognised me and cursed me by name. I smiled as I watched him bleed on the floor while his wife sobbed in the corner and his daughter turned glazed eyes up to the ceiling while the third man mounted her.

I didn't, at the time, draw the connection between what I was doing and what had been done to James, and it felt good. It felt right. Jones reminded me so much of my father, so much, that it felt right to watch him suffer. To hear him whimper as he lay on the floor of the house that slavery built, clutching his knee and pouring his life out onto the ground.

Later, when the boys were done with his women they left them there, in the house, and dragged Jones out to the farm-yard. They bound his hands, tied them to the saddle of his horse and it was me, me who slapped that nag's flank and sent it running out into the wild.

Me.

~~~

The days and nights were a blur then. Of whiskey and darkness. No one spoke to me, and why would they? The good men reviled me, rightly enough, and those of us who had done what we did at Fred Jones' homestead, well, we couldn't bear to look at one another in the light of a new day.

I drank at night, to numb, to forget, and in the morning I'd be sick from whiskey and shame. It was a cycle. A spiral I didn't know how to break out of. I didn't know if I deserved to.

Then John Gordon came and slapped me on the back. "Looks like you'll get your revenge," he said. "Word is we're heading out to your old man's place at dawn."

I'd been so lost in guilt and drink I hadn't even noticed that we were in the land around my father's homestead.

Something flared in my belly. Anticipation, blood lust. I would see my father bleeding on the floor. I would hear him beg as I grounded him the way he had me, but without the laudanum Abe's pity had bought. Then the thought of Abe killed my joy. I turned away from John and stalked off toward the edge of camp where I could be alone.

Father wasn't the only person on his homestead. Abe was there too. Abe and Amy. *Oh, Amy.*

I stayed out there, on the fringes of camp, kicking stones and staring off at the sunset. No one approached me and I could imagine why. My shoulders felt tight, my hands were fists. I wouldn't have wanted to come too close either, to risk becoming the target of my fury. Like Jones had. Like his daughter had.

Oh, Amy.

I imagined my father with the gun to his head, Abe sobbing in the corner while the Redlegs took turns with Amy. Poor sweet Amy.

I couldn't let that happen.

Once the camp was quiet and most of the men had gone to sleep I stole John Gordon's horse.

The penalty for horse theft is hanging, but I expect that doesn't matter. I'm a dead man anyway. If I live through this they'll shoot me for desertion or hang me for the horse. Either way, dead is dead.

I rode until I heard the hum of the generators that powered his fence. I can hear them now, can feel them pulsing in my chest. They tug at the iron there. Not quite painful, I'm too far away yet for that, but definitely present. Making themselves known.

I can't cross the fence with this iron in my chest. It's impossible. But that is where Amy is sleeping, innocent and unaware.

I dig my heels cruelly into the horse's sides and it leaps forward, moving at a dead run through the magnetic fence line. I am going to cross the magnets, one way or another. I need to warn Amy.

*Three days, can you imagine?* John's words repeat in my skull, echoing like the reverberations from a fireball. I don't need three days, just a few minutes.

A storm is coming.

# ABOUT THE AUTHOR

Rhonda Parrish is driven by a desire to do All The Things. She founded and ran Niteblade Magazine, is an Assistant Editor at World Weaver Press and is the editor of several anthologies including, most recently, *Fire: Demons, Dragons and Djinn* and *E is for Evil*.

In addition, Rhonda is a writer whose work has been in publications such as *Tesseracts 17: Speculating Canada from Coast to Coast* and *Imaginarium: The Best Canadian Speculative Writing* (2012 & 2015). Her YA Thriller, *Hollow*, is forthcoming from Tyche Books.

Her website, updated weekly, is at
http://www.rhondaparrish.com

# ACKNOWLEDGEMENTS

"The Other Side of the Door" was originally published in *Kzine Issue #8*, January 21, 2014

"Cold Comfort" was originally shared on RhondaParrish.com in December 2013

"A Voice Too Many" is original to this collection

"A Million Pieces" was originally shared on RhondaParrish.com in December 2014

"Coming Storm" was originally published by *Shroud Magazine* in April 2014

**Download your FREE copy of Rhonda's award-winning post-apocalyptic short story, "Starry Night" now!**

**Click (or tap) Here**

or visit https://dl.bookfunnel.com/27vrtp1z8y

# Always Be The First
# To Know!

Whether it's a new release, a call for submissions, cover reveal, super sale or I just want to share a new story I've written, you will always be among the first to know if you sign up for my mailing list.

I promise to respect your privacy and your inbox. I will only email you when I have something exciting to share, probably about twice a month.

## Subscribe to Rhonda's Mailing List!

http://eepurl.com/cXoF5P

## Aphanasian Stories

Three of Rhonda Parrish's beloved Aphanasian stories in one collection for the first time!

A Love Story: Z'thandra, a swamp elf living with the Reptar, discovers a human near the village. When she falls in love with him, she faces a decision that will affect the Reptar for generations.

Lost and Found: Xavier, the escaped subject of a madman's experiments, and Colby, a young lady on a mission to save her brother, combine their efforts to elude capture and recover the magical artifact that will save Colby's brother.

Sister Margaret: A vampire hunter and a half-incubus swordsman are hired by a priestess to kill the undead pimp that is extorting, torturing and murdering vulnerable girls..

**Haunted Hospitals** (co-authored with Mark Leslie)

A look inside the hospitals, asylums, and sanatoriums in which formal spectral residents refuse to move on.

Hospitals are supposed to be places of healing, places of birth, and places of hope. But with all of the varying highs and lows that are experienced in these buildings, is it any wonder when echoes linger indefinitely? How about asylums, which house some of society's worst offenders and troubled inmates, or sanatoriums, places where the mentally and physically ill find themselves trapped, even after death?

Journey inside the history of these macabre settings and learn about the horrors from the past that live on in these frighteningly eerie tales from Canada, the United States, and around the world.

## Waste Not (And Other Funny Zombie Stories)

This collection of three funny zombie stories nods to the tradition of combining zombies and humor and continues it.

Waste Not - The coming of zombies forces humankind back to the land, to a simple lifestyle where 'Waste Not, Want Not' becomes more than a motto, it becomes the key to survival. And revenge.

Feeders - The zombie apocalypse will affect more than just humans, explore the repercussions of walking dead through the eyes of a cat in this story guaranteed to make you smile.

...Oh My! - What if the Wicked Witch of the West wasn't killed by Dorothy's house? What if she couldn't be, because she was a zombie. Dun dun dun!

## White Noise — Poetry from the Zombie Apocalypse

Watch the end of the world unfold in these twenty zombie-tastic poems by Rhonda Parrish. Experience the grime and the gore of the shambling, undead menace right alongside moments of hope and love.

"A collection of vivid scenes laid out in sharp and articulate verse, that when assembled, construct a grim narrative filled with tension, stark imagery, and unusual beauty. WHITE NOISE reaches in and evokes a visceral response— not always the one you'd expect."

—Tim Deal, Shroud Quarterly

.